SNOW
BEAR

For Daniel and Nicholas

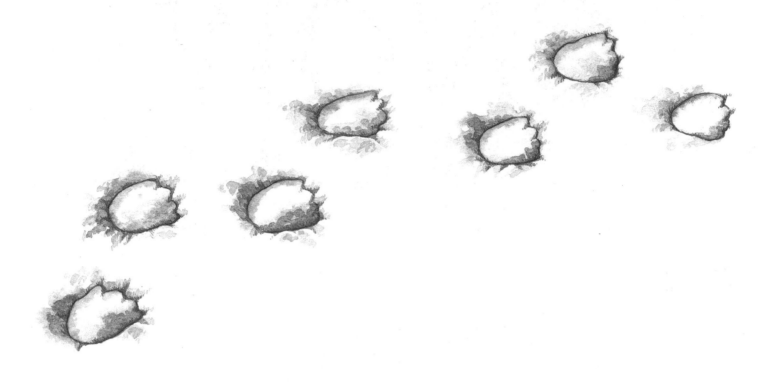

Published by Bonney Press,
an imprint of Hinkler Books Pty Ltd
45–55 Fairchild Street
Heatherton Victoria 3202 Australia
www.hinkler.com.au

BONNEY
PRESS

Originally published by Fernleigh Books, London

© Cat's Pyjamas 2012
Text © Fernleigh Books 2002
Illustrations © Piers Harper 2002

Prepress: Graphic Print Group

ISBN: 978 1 7430 8839 5

Printed and bound in China

SNOW BEAR

Piers Harper

BONNEY
PRESS

Little Snow Bear had been snuggled up with his mother all winter inside their cosy den. He was longing to go outside.

On the first day of spring, his mother said, "It's time for you to meet the world, my little one."

Little Snow Bear rolled around in the soft, powdery snow. It was so much fun, he did it again and again!

"Now you can go and explore," said his mother. "But stay by the water's edge where I can see you. I don't want you getting lost."

Little Snow Bear ran down to the water. It was blue and shimmery—the most beautiful thing he had ever seen.

He saw something swimming in the water, making it ripple and splash. So he went to take a closer look.

"Hello," said a little seal. "Do you want to come play with me?"
The water looked so exciting that Little Snow Bear jumped
right in—*SPLASH!* Exploring was so much fun!

Little Snow Bear had a great time playing splashing games with his new friend. Soon he remembered what his mother had said about getting lost. He looked around, but he did not see her anywhere. He got out of the water and shook himself dry. "Good-bye," he said to the little seal, and he set off to find his mother.

Little Snow Bear padded across the ice, but he soon found himself in a big forest. He was just starting to feel a little worried when he heard a friendly voice.

"Hello there," said a reindeer. "What are you doing here all alone?"

"I'm exploring," said Little Snow Bear. "But now I need to find my mother."

"Come with me," said the reindeer kindly.
"I'll show you the way out of the forest."

Once outside the forest, Little Snow Bear was sure his mother would be waiting ... but she was not there! Suddenly exploring was not so much fun. His tummy rumbled. He felt hungry.

Nearby, Little Snow Bear saw a little girl fishing.

"Hello," said the little girl. "What are doing out here all alone?"

"I was exploring," Little Snow Bear said, sniffling. "But now I'm hungry. I'm tired and I'm lost—and I want my mother."

"Getting lost is no fun at all,"
said the little girl. "Don't worry.
I'll help you find your mother.
But first, I will give you
something to eat."

After eating a delicious fish meal, Little Snow Bear climbed into the girl's sled. "Come on," she said to her dogs. "Let's take this Little Snow Bear home." And off they sped across the snow.

"There she is!" Little Snow Bear saw his mother and ran to her.

"Where have you been?" she asked. "I've been so worried about you."

"I'm sorry I got lost," said Little Snow Bear.

"I'm so happy that you're home safe," said his mother.

Little Snow Bear began to tell her all about his adventure.

His mother gave him a big hug.
"I love you, my Little Snow Bear," she whispered
as he fell fast asleep, safe in her arms.